AN

S.

Illustrat

Hutchinson
London Melbourne Auckland Johannesburg

aura was seven years old. She lived with her family in the end house in the small village of Lark Rise. In a shed in the garden lived the Dinner Pig. Once a year he provided a huge feast, and enough bacon to last all year round, and then another pig would arrive. But each Dinner Pig was a friendly and attentive listener.

Laura had a younger brother called Edmund, who was very clever. Laura knew their mother loved both of them just the same, but that didn't stop her feeling a bit jealous.

For a long time, Laura was the only one from the end house who went to school, because she was the eldest. Edmund would stay behind to play, and read stories with their mother. But one day at tea, Laura's mother said to her

father: "It's a big day tomorrow. Edmund starts school!"

Laura looked across the table at her brother, whose cheeks were bulging. He had too much in his mouth, but Laura's mother did not seem to notice. Instead she said:

"You be a good boy and work hard, Edmund. We expect great things of you."

Both parents smiled. Laura scowled.

"Don't make that face, Laura," said her mother. "What if the wind changes?" Laura stopped scowling, and Edmund put his tongue out at her. The tongue had soggy crumbs stuck to it, and did not look pretty.

After tea, to put the thought of tomorrow out of her mind, Laura went round the rise, to see who she could see. The first person she met was her best friend Ella May Sowerby, who was on the green where the bad-tempered white geese waddled and pecked among the dandelions.

Ella May was big for her age. She was skipping – THUMP dot, THUMP dot. . .

"Hallo . . . Laura . . ." she said. "Schoolter . . . morrow . . ."

"I know," said Laura gloomily. "Edmund starts."

"Wanto . . . join in?" asked Ella May. Laura ducked in under the rope.

"I wouldn't . . . mind if . . . he wasn't . . . so clever . . ." said Laura, using up rather a lot of breath.

"Well——!" gasped Ella May, coming to the end of hers and collapsing on the grass, "being clever's not everything."

As she continued round the rise Laura reflected that while it might not be everything, it was certainly a fairly large something.

She went a little way out of the village till she reached the cottage of Old Sally. She could see Old Sally in the garden, picking beans in her white apron and big floppy sun bonnet. As soon as she spotted Laura by the gate she came over.

 "Good evening, my dear," she said, rubbing Laura's cheek with her warm, dry finger. "Why are you so down in the mouth?"

"Edmund starts school tomorrow," said Laura. She felt rather silly. She didn't want to say anything nasty about Edmund – it wasn't his fault he was clever – but she knew her reason sounded silly on its own.

But Old Sally was wise. "Don't you worry," she said, "it won't be so bad. Here, take some beans home for your mother."

Laura set off home, carrying the bundle of beans wrapped up in paper. Far away down the road she could see the tall trees and the church spire of the next village, where the school was. That night she added an extra prayer to all her usual ones: "Please God don't let me be shown up by Edmund."

Next morning they were all up early, and a great fuss was made over Edmund. While his hair was being flattened with water, and his jacket brushed and buttoned, Laura went out to the pigsty.

"I'm not looking forward to today," she confessed to the Dinner Pig. "It's going to be awkward having a younger brother who's good at things." The Dinner Pig twitched his flat pig snout at her and waggled his rubber corkscrew of a tail.

"And I suppose I'll have to look after him all day," added Laura grumpily.

"Laura!" called her mother. "Hurry up, and stop talking to yourself."

Laura trailed into the cottage.

"I want you to look after your brother," went on her mother. "No misbehaving. Don't let the big boys be rough with him, and watch this new jacket doesn't get spoilt." And with a last tweak and a pat she ushered them out of the front door.

Laura trudged at a steady pace, while Edmund rushed and dawdled by turns. Ella May fell in step beside Laura.

"Where's your brother?" asked Ella May.

"Somewhere about," said Laura.

"Oh yes," said Ella May. And then: "Oh dear. He's with Davey Meekins."

Davey Meekins was the nastiest boy in Lark Rise, and by far the biggest. He was big upwards, and big across and big

around, with small beady eyes and an upturned nose with nostrils on the front of it, like a pig's. In fact, Davey Meekins looked remarkably like the Dinner Pig, but not nearly so friendly and intelligent. He had grabbed Edmund by the lapels of his new jacket, and pulled him up on his toes.

"New boy, is it?" he was asking in a squeaky, sneering voice. "Just a little 'un, aren't you? Just a mummy's boy in 'is smart new jacket." And with that he gave Edmund a shake, like a terrier with a rat, and dropped him to the ground where he landed with a resounding thump!

Davey Meekins smirked, and strolled away with his hands in his pockets.

"That wasn't too bad," said Ella May, a little disappointed.

"Still, I'd better go and check," sighed Laura, and went over to Edmund. There was no blood that she could see, and the jacket was all right, thank goodness.

"Now then, Edmund," she said, "you'd–"

But Edmund was not listening. His face was crimson, his eyes were bulging from his head and his fists were clenched. All in all he did not look one bit like Edmund, the apple of his mother's eye, of whom great things were expected.

"HEY, YOU!" he bawled after Davey Meakins. "YOU, PIG-FACE!"

Laura gaped. Davey Meekins turned round. And so did everyone else. School was forgotten. No one wanted to miss this.

"Did you call me, pip-squeak," asked Davey Meekins, his eyebrows drawing together in one long, furry caterpillar.

"Yes, I did!" yelled Edmund, "Glad you know your name, pig-face!"

Laura and Ella May looked at each other. Laura gulped. She put her hand on Edmund's arm and said, "Come along, Edmund."

But Edmund just pushed her away without even looking at her. He marched right up to Davey Meekins, pulling off his jacket as he went, and before Davey could even get his fists up he was wading into him.

Edmund's arms, with tightly clenched fists on the end, went round and round like the spokes of two small wheels, and his hard boots crunched on Davey Meekins' shins. Unfortunately, every time the boots came down they trampled on the nice new jacket, crumpling it and tearing it and driving it deep into the muddy ruts in the road. Davey Meekins was only a bully, and not very brave. Also, he was too fat to move quickly. He soon lost his balance, rocked backwards, tried to recover, and finally pitched forward – whump! – at Edmund's feet.

"Well I never!" gasped Ella May, under her breath. "Your little brother, fancy!"

The other boys gave Edmund a cheer, and he waved to them. Then he bent down and grabbed the sleeve of his jacket, which stuck out from beneath Davey, and gave it a tug. The sleeve came off in his hand. Laura closed her eyes.

After that, the rest of Edmund's first day at school was very dull. The teacher, Miss Holmes, was not too hard on him for fighting, because he was new, and anyway she knew all about horrible Davey Meekins. Laura had rolled up the jacket as small as she could and stuffed it in her bag.

On the way home Edmund sidled up to her.

"I'm sorry about the jacket," he said. "What will mother say?"

"I don't know," replied Laura grimly. "I shall have to think of a plan."

All the way back to Lark Rise Edmund walked just a little behind Laura. A very different Edmund to the one who had rushed up and down early this morning, and who had thumped Davey Meekins.

As they approached the end house they could see their mother sitting in the window, sewing. When she saw them she put down the sewing, and came to the front door to meet them.

"Where's Edmund's new jacket?" she asked, straight away.

Laura opened her school bag and took out the torn and muddy jacket, and the ripped-off sleeve. "You mustn't be cross," she said, as her mother looked with a white face at the two sorry-looking rags. "That beastly Davey Meekins attacked Edmund!"

"What?" Laura's mother sounded quite bemused.

"And Edmund was *wonderful*," added Laura, making the most of it. "He stuck up for himself, and in the end Davey Meekins ran away, and everyone cheered, and he probably won't bully anyone ever again!"

She ran out of breath and stared, pink-faced and anxious, at her mother. Edmund stared at the front step. Their mother stared at each of them in turn.

Laura had told the truth, but not every bit of it. She did not say that Edmund had picked a fight with Davey. Nor that he'd pulled off the new jacket and thrown it on the ground. Nor that he'd ripped the sleeve away while showing off.

The staring seemed to go on for a long time, Laura felt so hot and bothered she half-expected smoke to come out of her ears. Then all of a sudden her mother tucked the mucky jacket under her arm, and gave first Laura, then Edmund, a tight, brisk hug.

"Very well," she said. "We'll forget it. I'll see what I can do with the jacket. Now come in and wash before tea."

As the children went into the house after her, Edmund caught Laura's hand and gave it a fierce squeeze.

"Thank you, Laura," he whispered. "You saved me."

And just for once Laura felt brave, and grown up – and thoroughly superior.